Ghost Stadium

For Thomas Macartney

First published in 2013 in Great Britain by
Barrington Stoke Ltd
18 Walker Street, Edinburgh, EH3 7LP

www.barringtonstoke.co.uk

Reprinted 2014, 2016

A CIP catalogue record for this book is available
from the British Library upon request

ISBN: 978-1-78112-227-3

Printed in China by Leo

Ghost Stadium

Tom Palmer

Chapter 1

The End

Three Year 9 boys walked out of the gates of their high school. They kept a fast pace, matching each other step for step.

Lucas, Jack and Irfan had something to do.

Something exciting.

Something risky.

And they wanted to get started as soon as possible.

Chapter 2

School's Out

The rest of the kids were in less of a hurry to leave school than Lucas, Irfan and Jack. In fact, today was the only day in the year that many of them would hang around the car park and the sports field instead of rushing off.

They chatted.

They laughed.

They signed each other's shirts.

It was the last day of the school year.

Summer!

Jack looked up at Lucas as they passed the crowds at the gate. "Is your mum going to be in?" he asked.

"No," Lucas said. "I told you. She flew out to Tenerife with her boyfriend before I left for school this morning."

Irfan smiled and ran his hand through his short dark hair. "So nobody will know we're not at your house tonight?" he asked.

"Nobody," Lucas said.

"And did you find your dad's old camping gear?" Irfan asked.

Lucas nodded. "I did."

"So we're on?" Jack asked.

"We're on." Lucas smiled. "We take the tent and three sleeping bags. We pick up some food from the supermarket. Then we go in."

Irfan shook his head. "I can't believe we're actually going to do this," he said.

Chapter 3

8-foot Fence

Later that night, the three boys stood in the shadow of an old football stadium. They put down their camping gear and shopping bags on the ground.

From here, they could see a huge wall of corrugated iron, massive columns of crumbling concrete and heaps of scattered rubble. It was all surrounded by an 8-foot-high fence.

Lucas's voice was low and quiet when he spoke. "Do you remember coming here to watch the football?" he asked.

Jack nodded.

"Like it was yesterday," Irfan said.

But it hadn't been yesterday. In fact, the last time the boys had been inside Northface Stadium was five years ago. On the final match day of the final season Yorkshire County FC ever played. Before the club was shut down and the stadium closed to players and fans.

It had been like this ever since. Falling apart, bit by bit. Overgrown with trees and bushes. Slowly claimed back by grass and moss.

The three boys turned when they heard the scream of a train passing into the city station a few streets away. The sound of its horn echoed around the old stadium.

"Come on," Lucas said. "Let's get in there. The longer we hang about here, the more chance someone will spot us going in."

Chapter 4

Illegal Entry

The boys used a long piece of iron to lever one of the sections of fence out from its base.

They worked as a team, in silence. But Lucas's mind wasn't quiet. In his memory he played back all the times he'd come here with his dad to watch Yorkshire County FC. He remembered the day his favourite football team had closed their doors for the last time. The fans had been told the stadium would be demolished in two weeks' time to make way for a supermarket. And then Lucas's favourite player

– Tommy Baird – had been found dead in the stadium. No one knew what had happened.

Lucas kept his memories to himself as they replaced the fence panel to look as if it had not been touched. They moved with care so as not to make any noise, even though they knew they were alone. Then Lucas led Irfan and Jack towards the old turnstiles.

What they saw was a great disappointment to them. Every turnstile entrance was sealed off with a huge sheet of iron, bolted from inside, just like some of the old pubs and shops in the city that had been closed down.

It was impossible to get in.

"So what are we going to do now?" Jack asked.

Chapter 5

How to Break Into a Football Stadium

After twenty minutes of scouting the area, the lads had worked out that there was only one way to get in.

There was no way they could climb the walls.

It was impossible to break down the doors.

And they didn't want to smash any windows.

None of those was an option.

But there was one thing they could try. The legs of the old footlights straddled the corner of the stadium – half inside the walls, half out. They could climb up one of those, then come back down on the other side. It looked dangerous – and it was – but it was the only way of getting in without doing any damage. The only way that didn't feel too wrong.

Lucas went first. He'd done climbing with the Scouts and he knew the way to do it. He knew you always have three of your limbs in a secure position. Then you move the other one. That's the idea.

He concentrated hard as he began to climb.

Jack and Irfan watched in silence. They were afraid that if they spoke to Lucas it would break a spell and Lucas would fall.

"Why are we doing this?" Jack whispered, as Lucas nearly slipped and fell. He was at least two metres above them now.

"Shut up," Irfan muttered. "It'll be OK."

After a minute Lucas was higher than the wall. At last he had a view of the inside of Northface Stadium. He was amazed at what he saw.

Chapter 6

Forgotten World

"It's still there," Lucas shouted down to the others. "The pitch! And all the stands. I mean ... it's a mess, but most things are in the same place."

It was an amazing sight. A football stadium that had been shut off for five years. Nothing had changed, apart from what nature had done.

Lucas shifted his attention back to his climb. Now he could see there was a fixed ladder that reached from the pitch side to the lights at the top.

"There's a ladder here," he told the others. "Once you're up and over, it's easy."

Lucas climbed down the floodlight on the ladder, taking care his feet didn't slip on the thin metal rungs.

When he was down on the far side, he called to the others. "I'm in. Are you still there?"

Two voices called back. "Yes."

Lucas could sense fear in both the voices. What they were doing was dangerous and – if it went wrong – stupid. So he was all the more determined that nothing would go wrong. And the best way to make sure of that was to get on with it.

Chapter 7

The Drop

"Jack, you come next," Lucas shouted. "Just take your time as you climb, then edge across. I can direct you once I can see you."

"OK," he heard Jack call.

"Throw the gear over first, OK?" Lucas added.

There were a few scuffles and bangs and then the tent bag came over. It caught on the glass on the top of the breeze-block wall, then tumbled over to land at Lucas's feet.

Next came the three sleeping bags.

"We'll carry the rucksacks on our backs," Irfan called over. "The food's in those. We don't want to ruin it."

"Good plan," Lucas agreed.

As Jack began his climb the wall blocked him from Lucas's view. But then Lucas saw his hands appear above the wall, then his white T-shirt, then his legs. Jack was looking down at first, but then he raised his head and Lucas could see his face.

That was when Lucas knew there would be problems.

Jack's eyes looked huge, as if he was about to cry.

"I hate heights." He spat the words out like a child having a tantrum.

Lucas knew he had to handle this well. His friend would be OK unless he panicked. But now he was panicking. "Stay calm," Lucas said. "Just stay c – "

Lucas watched in horror as one of Jack's hands slipped. Now his legs were dangling over the broken glass on top of the wall.

"No!" Lucas said to himself. "This can't happen!"

He had to take control.

But as he opened his mouth to shout to Jack, he saw something else.

A flicker in the corner of his eye.

A dark shape.

A shape that looked like a man falling.

Chapter 8

Dark Shape

Lucas looked back and saw that Jack had steadied himself. Both of his feet were on the frame of the floodlight now.

"Are you OK?" Lucas shouted. His voice echoed back from the empty football stands.

"Fine." Jack's voice was shaky.

"Just take one step at a time," Lucas told him. "OK?"

"OK."

Lucas watched his friend edge across to the ladder and descend step by step. Even from the ground it was obvious that his legs were shaking.

Lucas helped Jack down the last few steps with a hand on his back. "You did well there," he said. He wanted to make Jack feel better about what had just happened.

Jack smiled.

Soon Irfan had joined them inside the stadium. The three boys stood and gazed at the wasteland of trees and bushes that now grew on what had once been a Premier League football pitch. Pieces of iron swung down from the four empty stands.

Lucas's mind kept going back to the black shape he had seen falling. He wished he could work out what it had been.

He could only think that it had been a bird like a swift or a swallow. Possibly a bat. Or a larger bird. Maybe it had been something falling off the top of one of the stands? A small piece of metal, rusted and torn?

But it had seemed bigger than that. Much bigger.

Things must fall off the stadium all the time, he thought. In the night. During the day. A thousand pieces of this old stadium must have come down in the last five years. Maybe more.

It had to be something like that. There was no way it could have been what Lucas really thought he had seen.

Chapter 9

Shadows

"This is unreal." Irfan's voice broke the silence and Lucas's train of thought.

It was unreal. Very unreal. Nature had been allowed to take over the football pitch, the stands, the stone, the metal. The plants and rain had almost returned it to a wilderness.

It had been a sunny day, but the evening heat and light had not made it into the stadium. The high walls made a shadow that would last until morning. There was no way for light to get in.

The tent pegs jingled on the ground as Lucas began to pull the tent out of its bag. He wanted to get things set up straight away. Then they could explore.

"I don't like it here," Jack said all of a sudden. Lucas was angry – that was no way to start an adventure.

"You're just a bit shocked," Irfan comforted him. "You nearly fell."

Lucas ignored them both. "Where shall we pitch the tent?" he asked.

"It'll have to be here," Irfan said. "It's the only place that's really flat."

Irfan was right. The rest of the pitch was a forest of long grass, bushes and small trees. There was just one flat area under the floodlight.

"Happy here, Jack?" Lucas asked. He was aware of Jack looking at the wall they'd just climbed, as if he was thinking about leaving.

Jack nodded. "Suppose so," he said. "How do we get out tomorrow morning?"

Lucas smiled. "I'll find a way, Jack. Now we're in it'll be easy to get out. There'll be a door that opens from the inside. I promise."

Jack frowned, but said, "OK."

"Really, it'll be fine," Lucas repeated.

"I said 'OK'," Jack snapped.

Chapter 10

Dead Wood

"Right, let's set up camp," Lucas said. He tried to sound keen, to break the strain they were feeling thanks to Jack's bad mood.

Lucas knew he needed to get back the high they'd been on when they came out of school. This trip was a big deal. They'd been planning it for months. Jack was putting a dampener on everything and Lucas wanted to stamp that out.

Irfan seemed to want to improve the mood too. "I can't believe we've got six weeks off school," he said. "This is such a good way to kick it off."

Jack knelt down to help, taking poles and pegs, waiting for Lucas to tell him what to do.

"I'll go and find some wood," Irfan said. "Maybe some old seats or something. We should start a fire."

And with that, Irfan made off across the pitch, taking careful steps to avoid rabbit holes and big chunks of concrete and iron that had fallen off the stadium.

For the next couple of hours the boys sorted their camp. Now they were used to the stadium, they began to have fun.

But that was about to change.

Chapter 11

Horror Stories

By 9pm the tent was up, the fire was burning well, and the three boys were sitting round in the warm. Their sandwiches were long gone. Now they were finishing off the giant family cake and Coke they'd bought at the supermarket.

Night was falling.

Over the last two hours, the boys had talked and laughed – and sometimes they'd stayed silent and just watched.

Jack had spotted a fox on the far side of the stadium. It had sat half way up the west stand

and watched them. They had gone after it to get a closer look, but it disappeared the moment they reached the stand.

Also there were hundreds of birds. Swifts and swallows, thrushes and sparrows, swooping over the grass in search of flies. It was like being in the countryside, miles away from the city. Hard to believe they were five minutes' walk from one of the biggest shopping centres in the country.

In the silence – and while Irfan was checking his iPhone – Jack pulled a book out of his bag.

"Darren Shan?" Lucas spluttered. "I didn't know you were a horror reader."

Jack just grinned.

"Do you like zombie books?" Irfan asked. He put his iPhone down and leant forward to look at the cover of Jack's book.

"Yeah!"

"Me too," Irfan said. "*The Fear*. All those Charlie Higson ones. They creep me out."

"They're pretty scary," Jack said. He seemed totally calm now. Lucas was pleased he'd relaxed.

"'Pretty scary'?" Irfan repeated. "What about the bit in *The Enemy*, where that couple catch the boy in the underground and go to eat him?"

Jack grinned and waved his Darren Shan book. "These are more scary."

"You want scary?" Lucas asked.

"Go on then," Jack laughed.

"Are you sure you can handle it?"

"'Course," Jack said. But his smile had gone.

Chapter 12

Death by Misadventure

"Books can be spooky," Lucas said. "But it's real things that are the most scary."

"Rubbish!" Jack said.

"Rubbish?"

"Yeah. There's nothing real that's as scary as stuff in books."

"What about the thing that happened right here?" Lucas asked. "What happened to Tommy Baird? That's proper scary."

The noise came as soon as Lucas said the dead footballer's name. A loud clang, like a football hitting the back of the corrugated iron stand. Lucas immediately wished that he'd kept his thoughts to himself.

"Well done, Lucas," Irfan said, in a sharp voice. "You've woken the dead now."

Lucas looked at Jack as he waited for a remark from him, but Jack looked down at his book and avoided eye contact.

Lucas frowned. Tommy Baird was a subject that very few people raised in the city. It was too sad. But he'd started now. He had to go on.

Just before Yorkshire County FC closed down five years before, they had had a world class player. His name was Tommy Baird. He was 19 years old and – even though Yorkshire County FC were a League One team by then – he had already been in the England first team at the World Cup finals. People said that teams like Man U and Chelsea were looking at him. Even Barcelona.

But Tommy Baird had died.

In an accident.

In this stadium.

Nobody knew what really happened to him. Nobody was charged with any crime. The police inquest called it 'death by misadventure'.

But Tommy Baird's death had started a chain of events that meant that Yorkshire County FC had ceased to exist.

Chapter 13

Changing the Subject

"What other kinds of books do you like?" Lucas asked Jack. He wanted to change the atmosphere that he had caused by talking about Tommy Baird. It was almost as if the air had gone colder. He could feel the hairs on the backs of his arms prickle his skin.

"All sorts," Jack said. He stood up and shifted about. "I need the loo."

Lucas and Irfan turned to look the other way, as Jack walked into the longer grass to find a bush to go behind.

"I can't believe this is where we used to come to watch the football," Irfan said. It was clear he was trying to sound cheerful. "It looks so different."

Lucas nodded. "It's nice to come back one more time. Before they demolish it."

"Yeah," Irfan said.

"I wish someone had bought the stadium and started a new team. I miss it. A lot."

Just then they heard Jack coming back. "We should have a look round," he called. "Before it goes da – "

Jack stopped speaking at the same time as Lucas saw it again.

A black shape. Swooping. Or falling.

In between their camp and the main stand.

This time he could see it wasn't a bird. The shape was a man. Unmistakably a man.

Chapter 14

Lying

Lucas swallowed. "Did ... you ... see ... that?" he asked.

"Yes," Irfan stuttered.

They looked round to see Jack standing still in the long grass.

"I saw it too," Jack said.

All of a sudden the evening seemed much darker. The spaces at the back of the stands were voids of blackness. The only real light was coming from the sky and that was fading fast. Even the ground and grass in front of them seemed grey, not the burst of bright green they'd seen when they arrived.

"It must have been a bird swooping," Jack said. "Look at all the insects."

But Lucas shook his head. "What about the noise?" he asked. "When that thing hit the ground there was a thud." Lucas turned to Irfan. "Did you hear it?"

"That could have been anything," Jack went on. His voice was getting louder. "Something from outside. One of the factories? The motorway?"

"I saw it before," Lucas told them. "And I heard it before. When you were on the floodlight, Jack. Didn't you see it? You'd have had a perfect view. You must have. That's why you slipped."

"No, it wasn't. I slipped because it was a bloody stupid thing to do, climbing over that floodlight. That's why I slipped."

"No," Lucas pressed. "You saw it, didn't you?" He stepped towards Jack. "Admit it. You're lying."

Chapter 15

It Was a Bird

As the row between Lucas and Jack heated up, Irfan stepped forward to place himself between them.

"Maybe it's the stories we were telling each other," he said. He raised his eyebrows as he looked at Lucas. "We've worked ourselves up."

Lucas saw what Irfan was trying to tell him.

He was saying that Jack looked scared. Really scared.

What was the point in Lucas winding him up, just to prove a point?

"Look," Irfan went on, "we were sitting round the fire telling horror stories. It's getting dark. We're on our own. We're bound to start seeing things. And what if it was a big shadow falling down then disappearing? So what? It could be anything. We're here to have a good time. Let's go back to the fire and talk about what we're going to do this summer. We could plan another camping trip. Somewhere not so ... you know. How about it?"

Lucas put his hand on Jack's arm. He could feel how stiff his friend's muscles were. Stiff and tense.

"Irfan's right," he admitted. "I'm sorry, Jack. I was just trying to wind you up. I didn't see it before. It's just birds. Bats. Something like that."

Jack gave an eager nod. "A bird, I'd say. They move so fast. They're just a blur."

"Yes," Lucas said. He caught Irfan's eye. "A bird. It was just a bird."

Chapter 16

Hunted

The three friends walked through the long grass and back to the camp fire. Its flames were bright and colourful now, against the darker sky.

Lucas listened to Irfan talk away about plans for the future. How they could cycle to the seaside. Or up into the mountains. They had six weeks to do whatever they wanted.

But no matter how impressed Lucas was with Irfan for calming Jack down, he still couldn't shake the feeling that something was hunting them. It was a feeling that wouldn't go away.

He stared into the depths of each football stand, not sure what he was looking for. Then he looked up at the sky. All the birds seemed to be disappearing – they flew round the stadium, then left. Lucas caught a glimpse of the fox as it flashed through a hole in the wall. It was leaving too.

But Lucas comforted himself that the mood was calmer now. Jack looked happier now that he had convinced himself that it had been a bird.

"I need to get something out of the tent," Jack said. He went onto his hands and knees, shuffled about in his bag, then came out with a packet of cigarettes.

Jack thrust the packet at Lucas and Irfan. "Want one?" he asked.

Lucas shook his head.

Then it happened again.

Chapter 17

Not Just a Bird

This time they saw everything. There was no room for doubt. No way they could tell themselves it was just a bird.

A black shape fell. Slow at first, from the top of the floodlight, then faster. It hit the ground hard.

"Aaaargh!" Irfan yelled as he bolted for the flap of the tent. Jack was right behind him.

Then Lucas was inside too. His heart hammered as he did up the zip. Then he turned to see his two friends staring at him like he was the threat.

Lucas zipped the inner tent up too. But even as he did it, he wondered what the point was. What were a plastic zip and two sheets of thin waterproof fabric going to do to protect them?

And that was another problem. They had no idea what the threat was.

The three boys sat and stared at each other as they squatted on Jack's sleeping bag.

Lucas's mind was spinning with the memory of what he had seen. The shadow had not been a bird – it had been the shape of a man falling.

And Lucas knew exactly who that man was. But there was no way he was going to say it out loud.

None of them were.

But they were all thinking it. The shape was Tommy Baird. The footballer. Back from the dead.

That silence made it all the easier to hear the noise when it came again.

A man's body falling from a height, hitting the ground.

This time louder.

This time closer.

This time right outside their tent.

Chapter 18

The Collapse

Lucas, Irfan and Jack stared into each other's eyes, their faces lit from below by the torch.

The tent smelt musty and damp. Airless.

THUD.

That sound again. The black shape coming down again. Even though he could not see it, Lucas knew it was there. And that it was coming closer.

He looked at Jack, who had closed his eyes and gone rigid like he was in a coma.

A voice in Lucas's head was screaming at him. Get out! Get out! But he felt paralysed. It was like that feeling you get in a dream, when you want to run, but your body won't move.

THUD.

Again.

Louder still.

Closer.

Lucas knew it.

"We have to go," he said. He focused on Irfan, who wasn't so frozen with fear.

Irfan nodded.

Then, without a word, they grabbed one of Jack's arms each and started to pull him out of the tent. It was their only chance of doing something to stop all this horror. To get away.

That was when the tent collapsed.

On top of them.

Like a body had hit it.

Then the tent came down hard. The three boys were pinned to the ground by the weight that had fallen on top of them.

Chapter 19

Possessed

Breathless with terror, the three boys began to push back at whatever it was that had fallen on top of them. But the torch had spun to the far side of the tent. In the dark, it was impossible to see or do anything.

Lucas threw a couple of punches upwards. He had no idea if there was any point. Was he hitting at a tree? Or the shadow? It might even be one of his friends. He supposed it was just instinct to lash back at danger.

Irfan was thrashing about as well, nearer to the torch.

But now Lucas could hear that Jack's breathing was weird, like his windpipe was blocked.

And then he realised that there was no weight on them any more. No body. No tree. No whatever it was that had come down.

"The torch," he shouted.

"Here!" he heard Irfan reply. Irfan scrambled across the tent to reach it.

"Shine it on Jack," Lucas said. He tried to remember the things you had to do if someone was injured from his first aid course at Scouts. "He's choking."

The beam of the torch wobbled, hit the roof of the tent and then pointed straight at Jack's face. He was cowering at the far end of the tent. His knees were up to his chin and his arms were out in front, twitching like a boxer sparring.

"Jack," Lucas shouted. "It's OK. Jack."

"Jack!" Irfan echoed.

Lucas crawled to Jack and tried to take one of his wrists.

Jack's hand lashed out and struck Lucas on the chest. Lucas crashed back against the inside of the tent.

Chapter 20

Black Eyes

Lucas knew something terrifying was taking place.

The force with which he had been flung back was not what he would have expected from Jack. Jack had never had power like that before. He had never lashed out, had a fight or even hit anyone.

Lucas stared at the other boy in horror. His eyes were drawn to Jack's as they opened slowly.

But they were not Jack's eyes. They were shining, wet, black eyes. No pupils. No irises. No whites. Just never-ending blackness.

And now there was a smell. A terrible smell, like something electrical was burning. But stronger. So strong Lucas and Irfan choked, barely able to breathe.

They edged backwards at the same time.

They were cornered. They had no idea what was going to happen next. All they knew was that they were facing something so terrifying that it was beyond words, beyond normal feelings, beyond anything they had ever had to cope with before.

Chapter 21

The Voice of the Dead

Lucas pushed himself to the back of the tent. Irfan was doing the same. Lucas's eyes felt hot and his throat was dry.

Jack glared at them with his shining, brilliant, black eyes.

They had to get away from him.

The two boys made a move as one, lunging for the zipped flap behind their friend. They wanted to get out of the tent. It didn't matter what was out there. It couldn't be worse than it was in here.

But as they scrambled past, one each side of Jack, he snatched at their wrists. Lucas heard Irfan cry out in pain at the same time that he felt a grip like a vice on his own wrist. He rolled over onto his back as the grip twisted and found himself face to face with Irfan. The pain was extraordinary.

And the voice that spoke to them was not Jack's.

It was deeper, slower, darker, faster. And each word was like a punch to the head.

The two boys could do nothing but listen and tremble.

"No please ... Mr Chairman ... don't make me ... please ... I've changed my mind ... I'm not going to the press ... aaaarrggghhhhhhhhhh."

The tent came down on them again, but there was nothing they could do.

It was chaos.

It was terrifying.

They tried to curl their bodies to protect themselves, but their wrists were still held in that vice-like grip.

And now it was dark.

They heard movement, zips, scrambling.

Then silence.

They couldn't hear him.

They couldn't see him.

Lucas and Irfan realised that Jack had gone.

Chapter 22

Escape

"Come on!" Irfan got onto his knees in the tent and grabbed the torch. "He's gone. Let's get out of here."

"The fox hole," Lucas said.

"Yes."

Irfan led the way. They ran hard. Too hard. Their ankles twisted and strained as they ran across uneven ground torn up by animals and bushes. But it was the only way. They didn't even think about what they had just been through with Jack. There were no words.

As they ran, Lucas thought he saw a flicker over by the players' tunnel, like a figure disappearing inside. But he kept on running, too afraid to do anything but escape.

It took them just seconds to cross what had once been the football pitch.

Then they were back on concrete. Between the stands. They ran to the hole in the wall they'd seen the fox go through.

Irfan bent down and shone the torch to see where it led.

"The old car park!" he said. "Come on."

Then he stood aside to let Lucas go first.

Lucas tried to smile a thank you, but his lungs felt like they were going to burst after the run. It was hard to walk, let alone smile.

As they paused, their eyes met. Something passed between them, something that made them stop. They were about to leave their friend behind.

"Jack," Lucas said. "We can't leave him here."

"What?"

"We can't just leave Jack behind."

"I know," Irfan shook his head. "But it wasn't Jack. It was something … someone else."

"But it was still Jack," Lucas said.

They both peered back the way they had come.

"I saw him," Lucas confessed. "I think. He went under the main stand. Into the players' tunnel."

"You want to go back?" Irfan sounded horrified.

Lucas shook his head. "No."

"So let's get out of here."

Lucas didn't move.

Irfan looked at him. "We can't leave, can we?" he said.

"No," said Lucas.

Chapter 23

Into the Dark

It was not easy to walk down the players' tunnel and under the stand.

Irfan shone the torch into the void. The darkness came alive as the light made the fragments of wood and metal cast shadows on the walls.

Then something moved. A rabbit, its eyes lit up pink. It ran towards them, then spun and headed back the way it had come.

Lucas breathed in.

"Come on," he said. He could hear his own voice wobble.

And the two boys entered the black void beneath the main stand, with no idea of what would happen next, just sure it was the right thing to do.

There was only one corridor under the main stand. It ran the full length of the stand, with rooms off it every ten metres. Its white breeze-block walls were covered in strange brown stains, making shapes that sprang to life in Lucas's mind. Monsters. Ghosts. Demons. His mind played terrible tricks on him as rubbish, dead leaves and branches crunched under his feet.

They made themselves shine the torch into each and every room. Both their hearts were pounding hard. Both felt sick.

But it had to be done. They had to find Jack.

Chapter 24

The Third Room

The first room they came to still had a sign on the door.

AWAY DRESSING ROOM.

Irfan cast the torch around the room, his eyes half-closed with the fear of what they might find there.

The torch shone under the benches.

Into the showers.

Nothing there.

The next door was the referee's room. It was half-closed.

Lucas pushed it open, forcing a load of dead leaves and plants out of the way. The torch beam revealed only heaps of twigs and soil. Then Lucas put his hand on Irfan's arm. "Did you hear that?" he asked. Irfan jumped and turned the beam of the torch the way that they had come.

"What?"

The corridor was empty, apart from the awful shapes on the walls. "Upstairs," Lucas said. "He's upstairs."

"Do we go up there?" Irfan asked.

Lucas nodded. "Let's check the home dressing room first. Just to be sure he's not on this floor now. Then we'll go up."

Irfan nodded. They moved on to the next door, the third room, both of them sick with nerves. They were both asking themselves why they hadn't just run for it. But deep down they both knew they owed it to their friend to stay.

Lucas reached out to grip the door handle.

Chapter 25

How to Die

The handle to the home dressing room was stiff. Lucas had to twist hard to force it open. It made a loud crack that echoed up and down the inside of the football stand.

Then there was an echo from inside the room. Or a second noise. Lucas couldn't be sure.

He looked at Irfan.

Irfan nodded.

Lucas pushed the door.

Irfan cast the torch beam slowly around the room. Along the floor at first, then over an upside-down massage table, its stuffing bursting out in a dozen places. But there were no leaves on the floor. Only piles and patches of animal droppings.

Two or three mice – or maybe rats – skittered away in different directions, just as the torch beam caught a pair of trainers.

Irfan jerked the beam upwards.

A pair of legs.

A white T-shirt.

A face.

Then the beam shone straight into a pair of black eyes.

Jack's eyes.

Lucas and Irfan flinched back the second they saw him. But Jack did not move. He just stared at them.

Irfan kept the light on their friend. The smell of burning came again. It was so toxic they could hardly breathe. Then Jack's mouth began to move.

Chapter 26

The Voice

This time Jack didn't need to grip their wrists or twist them to the floor. It was enough that his black eyes were fixed on them. They were going nowhere and they knew it.

"We've got to get out of here. He knows I know. I've hidden the hard drive."

Lucas and Irfan glanced at each other. It was that weird voice again. Not Jack's. It was the voice of whoever or whatever had taken over his body.

"I've hidden the hard drive," not-Jack said.

"What does he mean?" Lucas asked.

"I don't know," Irfan whispered.

"I can hear voices. I can hear them talking," not-Jack said.

Lucas swallowed. This was the most terrifying situation he had ever been in. He didn't know if they'd survive this night. But deep inside he knew what he had to do. They had decided not to run away. They had come to rescue Jack.

And that was what they had to do.

Chapter 27

Tsunami

In the back of Lucas's mind he could hear a roaring sound like water. And the temperature was going up. Fast.

"It's us you hear talking, Jack," Lucas said. He tried to keep his voice steady. He didn't know if all these sounds and feelings they were experiencing were real or part of this haunting or possession or whatever it was. "It's me and Irfan," he said.

"I can hear them," not-Jack said. "I hid the hard drive in the massage table. Not in the office. They'll try and burn the hard drive."

"What hard drive?" Irfan asked.

"I can still hear them. But it's too quiet."

"WHAT HARD DRIVE?" Lucas shouted.

Jack twitched, but his eyes stayed on them. Black and shining and deep.

"It has all I need to get the chairman ousted," he said.

Lucas almost smiled. It was working. The thing inside Jack was talking to them.

"WE'LL DEAL WITH IT. I PROMISE!" Irfan said. He had to shout above the growing noise.

There were cracks.

Snaps.

A roaring like a tsunami wave was about to break over them.

"WE'LL DEAL WITH IT!" Irfan said again.

Jack looked at them. "Can I trust you? Will you see it through?"

"YOU CAN TRUST US, TOMMY!" Lucas said. Now he knew who it was he was really speaking to. "WE WILL SEE IT THROUGH."

Then two things happened at once.

Jack collapsed. His eyes went white, then they closed, and his body slumped on the tiled floor.

And there was a crash. The ceiling above them began to turn black and then there was a blast of heat as fire engulfed the building.

Chapter 28

Death Trap

Burning wood and brick burst through the ceiling and smoke filled their lungs. The heat was unbearable.

Lucas and Irfan leaped over the massage table and grabbed Jack. They pulled him off the floor and dragged him to the exit.

The corridor was lit by flames so the boys could see to find their way back to the players' tunnel and into the open air. They dragged Jack out onto the overgrown pitch.

They froze at the sight before them. The top half of the stand they had just been inside was in flames. As it collapsed, bright embers and smoke billowed high into the night sky.

They could just hear the noise of fire engine sirens above the roar of the fire.

Lucas almost collapsed with relief. They were not going to be alone for much longer. Help was on its way.

But then Jack's body went stiff again.

"The hard drive," he said, in that voice again.

Lucas looked down at him.

The eyes were back.

The black eyes.

As Lucas leapt back, Irfan cried out. Jack's hands were around his throat.

"The hard drive!"

Lucas jumped on top of Jack and tried to pull his hands from Irfan's throat, but Jack was too strong. His strength was not human.

"The hard drive!" he shouted again.

As Lucas pulled, he saw panic in Irfan's eyes. The life seemed to be draining away from him. Lucas punched and kicked Jack, but it had no effect. Jack was strangling Irfan. Killing him.

"Get the hard drive," that voice said again.

And Lucas realised that he had to retrieve the hard drive from the massage table in the home dressing room. That was the only way to stop Irfan being strangled. To save Jack from the thing that had possessed him.

Lucas turned to face the main stand. The fire was everywhere now, reaching out to set the other stands on fire too. Glass smashed and stonework fell. It was a scene from Hell.

But Lucas had to go back in there.

If he didn't, then both his friends could die.

Chapter 29

Heat

Lucas ran into the players' tunnel and under the stand before he could think the better of it.

He knew the floor above was burning. He knew the ceiling could collapse at any moment. But he also knew he had to get the hard drive.

If he didn't ... He couldn't even think about that.

As he turned left to enter the home dressing room, Lucas saw that what had been a black void a few minutes ago was now a bright wall of flame. The ceiling at the far end of the stand had collapsed.

Dark grey smoke was pouring along the top half of the tunnel towards Lucas, drawn to the clear air. But if he kept low, the air was clear. Just.

He had only seconds.

He ran.

As he reached the door to the home dressing room he could feel the intense heat of the flames at the end of the stand.

Was he too late?

Chapter 30

Instinct

Without a second's pause, Lucas darted into the dressing room. As he tried to rip the cover off the massage table, he heard creaks and groans and snaps from above. "COME ON!" he shouted, angry at himself for taking so long.

But no matter how hard he looked, he could find nothing inside the stuffing of the massage table.

When the dressing room ceiling caved in, Lucas leaped across the room.

It was instinct, and it saved his life.

The place where he had been standing a second before was now a heap of burning wood and carpet.

Lucas had failed.

He knew he had to make for the door now. It was too dangerous to wait. But it was only when he was half-way to the players' tunnel – and safety – that he realised he was dragging part of the massage table with him.

Instinct again.

Maybe he hadn't failed then?

Maybe ...

As he ran out from under the tunnel, Lucas heard a rip and a crash and felt a wave of heat.

Behind him, the stand caved in. The whole structure crumpled and collapsed as the fire swept through it.

But Lucas only had eyes for his two friends, both sitting on the grass beside their tent.

Both staring back at him.

Chapter 31

Bruised

Lucas had barely been aware of the sirens for the last few minutes.

It was only now that he really heard them.

Fire engines. Ambulances. Police cars.

"We should get out of here," Lucas said. He said it as much to see how his friends would react, as to get away from the fire.

Irfan nodded. "Yes." He stood up and rubbed his neck.

Lucas smiled. Irfan had bruises around his throat, but he looked OK.

That was good. Very good indeed.

But Jack looked dazed. Lucas still wasn't sure. Was Jack *Jack*, or was he still that other person? Lucas needed to see his eyes.

"Jack?" he said. "We should leave. It's dangerous here."

Jack carried on staring at the burning stand. Then he turned to face Lucas.

His eyes were bloodshot, but in every other way they were normal.

Lucas smiled again. Jack was back.

"Come on," he said. "Let's go."

Chapter 32

Police

The three boys squeezed through the hole they had seen the fox use. They left the massage table on the other side. It was impossible to bring that too.

Once they were outside, they could see the emergency vehicles to their left. The flashing lights lit up the old car park behind the stand. The sound of the fire and the huge water hoses and a helicopter high above them added to the chaos.

To the right there was darkness. Wasteland. An easy escape from this nightmare.

Irfan made to head into the darkness. But Lucas stopped him with a hand on his arm.

"What?" Irfan asked.

"We shouldn't run away," Lucas said. "We should tell them we were here."

Irfan shook his head. "They'll never believe us. They'll think we started the fire. We'll get blamed."

Jack stood in silence, leaning on the side of the stadium.

"They'll see us leaving," Lucas said. "They might already have spotted us from the helicopter. We should own up."

"No."

"Yes."

"No, Lucas. We'll get a police record. We'll be stuffed. We'll never get jobs. We'll end up in a Pupil Referral Unit."

"There's an ambulance," Lucas said. "We need to get Jack seen to."

Irfan looked at the ground and sighed. He didn't say anything for what seemed like ages.

"OK," he muttered at last.

The three boys began to walk towards the emergency vehicles.

Chapter 33

Truth

Lucas told the police the full story of their night as he sat next to Irfan in the back of a police car.

Jack was inside an ambulance being treated.

When Lucas had finished, the policewoman leading their interview put her notebook on the dashboard of her car. She turned to them.

"It's going to be hard to make that story stand up in court, lads," she said.

Lucas shook his head. "It's true."

"It's not, son. It's ..." she sighed. "It's crazy. If I didn't know better I would think that you'd been taking drugs." She peered into Lucas's eyes.

"What I don't understand is why you gave yourselves up," she went on. "Were you scared?"

"Not of you," Lucas said. "But yes. We were scared for our friend and for our lives."

The policewoman shook her head. "Breaking and entering. Arson. Wasting police time. Should I go on?"

A second policewoman opened the passenger door and climbed into the car.

"How's Jack?" Irfan asked her.

"Your friend? He's fine. Just a bit spaced out. But you've got a bigger problem now. The owner of the stadium has just shown up. And he doesn't look happy."

Chapter 34

The Killer

There was a loud bang as a fist came down on the roof of the police car.

One of the policewomen jumped out of the car.

"Please, sir," she said. "We are dealing with this."

But nothing would stop the man.

"Are these the little gits?" he demanded. He was short and grey-haired, wearing a long coat.

Lucas knew who the man was. It was Ben Cates, the former chairman and owner of Yorkshire County FC. Lucas had never liked him. He was one of those posh older men who made everyone else feel like they were rubbish.

But not today.

Lucas had seen into the mouth of Hell today already. A little man like this wasn't going to scare him after that.

"Sir." The policewoman raised her voice. "We have this in hand."

"They've destroyed my stadium," Ben Cates shouted.

"Your stadium?" Lucas snapped. He opened the door of the car and stood up to confront the older man. "You're the one letting this place rot," he said. "You're the one demolishing it so that you can build a supermarket. This is my stadium, my club …" The next sentence was out of Lucas's mouth before he knew it, but as soon as he said it, he knew it was true. "You're the one who killed To – "

Ben Cates broke in with an evil smile. "See over there?" he shouted, and pointed at a dark stone building with small windows.

"What?" Lucas asked.

"That's the Youth Offenders' Prison," Cates said. "You'll have a great view of the supermarket when it gets built. I hope you enjoy it."

Lucas felt himself being pushed back into the police car, a hand on his head.

He knew that what Ben Cates had said was right. He would end up in the young offenders' place. There was no way out of this. How could he prove that this man had killed Tommy Baird? How could he show that they had not caused the fire?

And then he knew.

"The hard drive," he said. "Tommy's hard drive."

Ben Cates's face went white.

"What?" his voice sounded choked, and he glanced around in panic.

Lucas turned to the policewoman. "Tommy Baird's hard drive. It's on the other side of that fence. Hidden in a massage table. It'll prove that Cates had a motive for killing Tommy."

Lucas looked up at Ben Cates to see how he had reacted to what he had said.

But Cates was gone. He was racing to the hole in the wall. Racing to get there before Lucas.

And Lucas knew he couldn't let that happen.

Chapter 35

Destroyed

Lucas scrambled over Irfan, who was still sitting in the seat next to him with his mouth open as he listened to everything that had been said.

Lucas pushed the door open, rolled onto the ground, then went after Ben Cates. Five years of football frustration drove him on.

"Come back!" one of the policewomen shouted. "Don't make it worse ..."

But Lucas was running.

He began to gain on the former football club owner.

Hard.

Fast.

Direct.

Lucas heard a siren going off. Shouts. A car skidding on the rough ground of the car park.

He leapt in front of Ben Cates and dived through the hole. The massage table was where he had left it minutes before.

He started to rip at the fabric cover.

Lucas had to find the hard drive before Cates or the police stopped him. He looked up for a second and saw that Ben Cates was halfway through the hole in the wall, but he was stuck, too fat to get through.

It gave Lucas the time he needed. He had the time to rip the cover off, tear the stuffing out of the table.

One minute.

Two minutes.

And then he found it.

A small black object.

A hard drive.

With information that would change everything ...

Chapter 36

Kicking Off

Just six months later Northface Stadium looked like a very different place.

The whole city had come together to make it happen.

Investors had invested.

Builders had built.

Volunteers had volunteered.

At 3pm Yorkshire County FC kicked off their first game for over five years.

They were playing in a lower league, ten tiers down from the last game they had played. But they were playing. And 30,000 fans had filled the three remaining stands to watch them.

After Lucas had handed the hard drive to the police, Cates had confessed to the murder of Tommy Baird. His nerves were shot. He told the police everything they wanted to know.

He told them that, for years, he had taken ticket sales and player transfer fees for himself. He'd cheated the fans and the club. The next move he planned was to sell the stadium to a supermarket for millions. But Baird had found some secret e-mails and had confronted Cates. That was the night Cates had murdered him.

The police still did not believe the story about the ghost. But Lucas, Irfan and Jack were only given warnings. No police record.

The fire service proved the fire had started in the old electrical system of the stadium. It was nothing to do with the boys.

But Lucas, Irfan and Jack were not in the stadium for this great occasion. They were on a hillside half a mile away, watching the match from there.

They'd sworn to each other that night: they'd never enter the Northface Stadium again.

It was a promise they would never break.

Thanks

Huge thanks to Wrexham Football Club for helping me to write this book by letting me camp on the pitch in their famous Racecourse Ground stadium. Especially to Lee Jones. Thanks too to my wife, Rebecca. And to everyone at Barrington Stoke for asking me – and helping me – to write it.